DC

TEEN TITANS GO! ™

ROBIN THE FIRST AND TEEN TITANS GO... FISH!

Teen Titans Go! is published by
Stone Arch Books,
A Capstone Imprint
1710 Roe Crest Drive
North Mankato, MN 56003
www.mycapstonepub.com

Library of Congress Cataloging-in-Publication Data is available at the Library of Congress website:
ISBN: 978-1-4965-7996-6 (library binding)
ISBN: 978-1-4965-8002-3 (eBook PDF)

Summary: Tired of finishing second, an ultra-competitive Robin comes up with a plan to show the rest of the Teen
Titans that he's actually the best. Then as the Teen Titans engage in an epic game of Go Fish, the Hive-Five come
knocking on their doorstep!

Alex Antone Editor – Original Series Paul Santos Editor

STONE ARCH BOOKS
Chris Harbo Editor
Brann Garvey Designer
Hilary Wacholz Art Director
Kathy McColley Production Specialist

Printed and bound in the USA
092019   002752

TEEN TITANS GO! ™

AMY WOLFRAM SHOLLY FISCH
WRITERS

JORGE CORONA CHRIS GUGLIOTTI
ARTISTS

WES ABBOTT
LETTERER

DAN HIPP
COVER ARTIST

STONE ARCH BOOKS
a capstone imprint

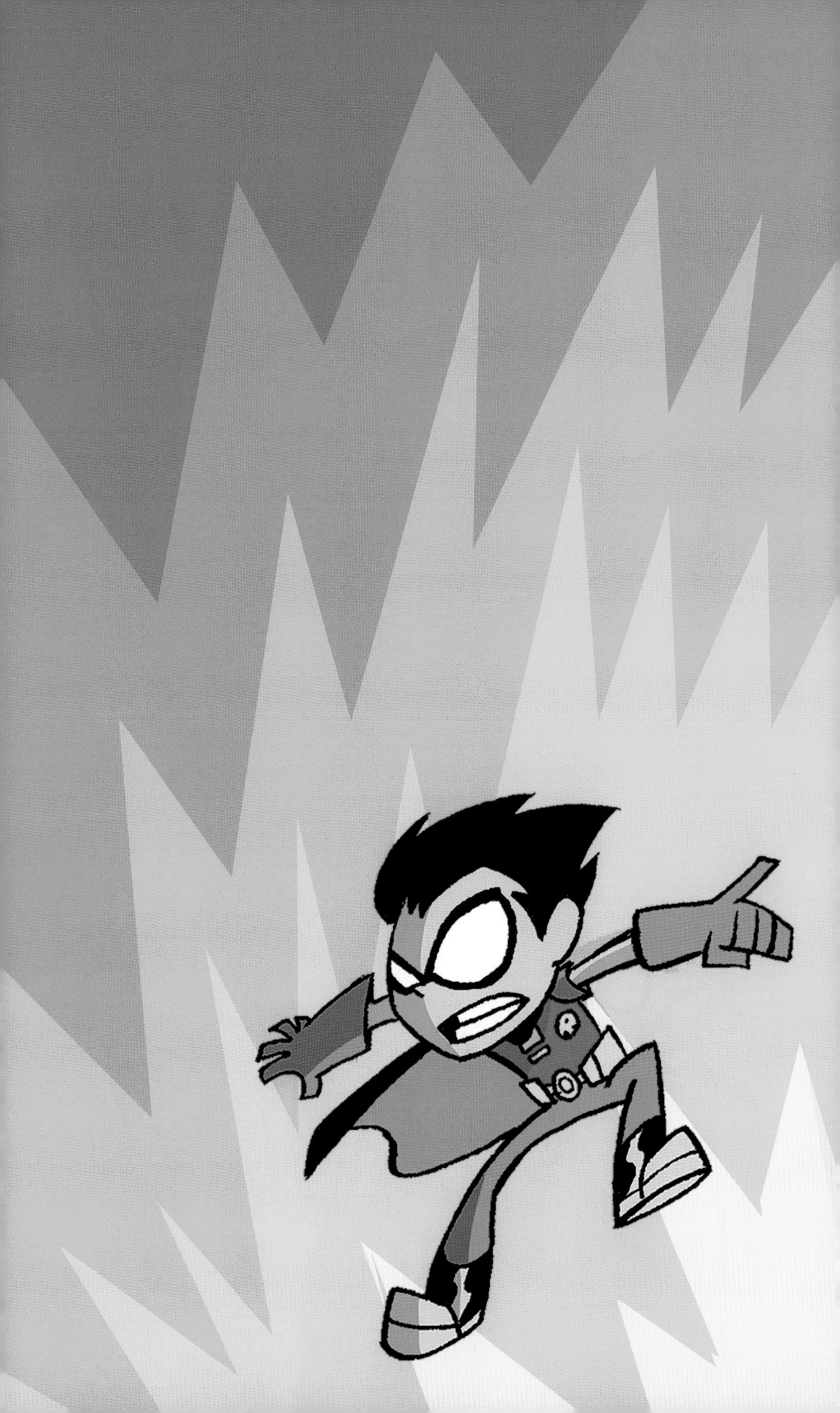

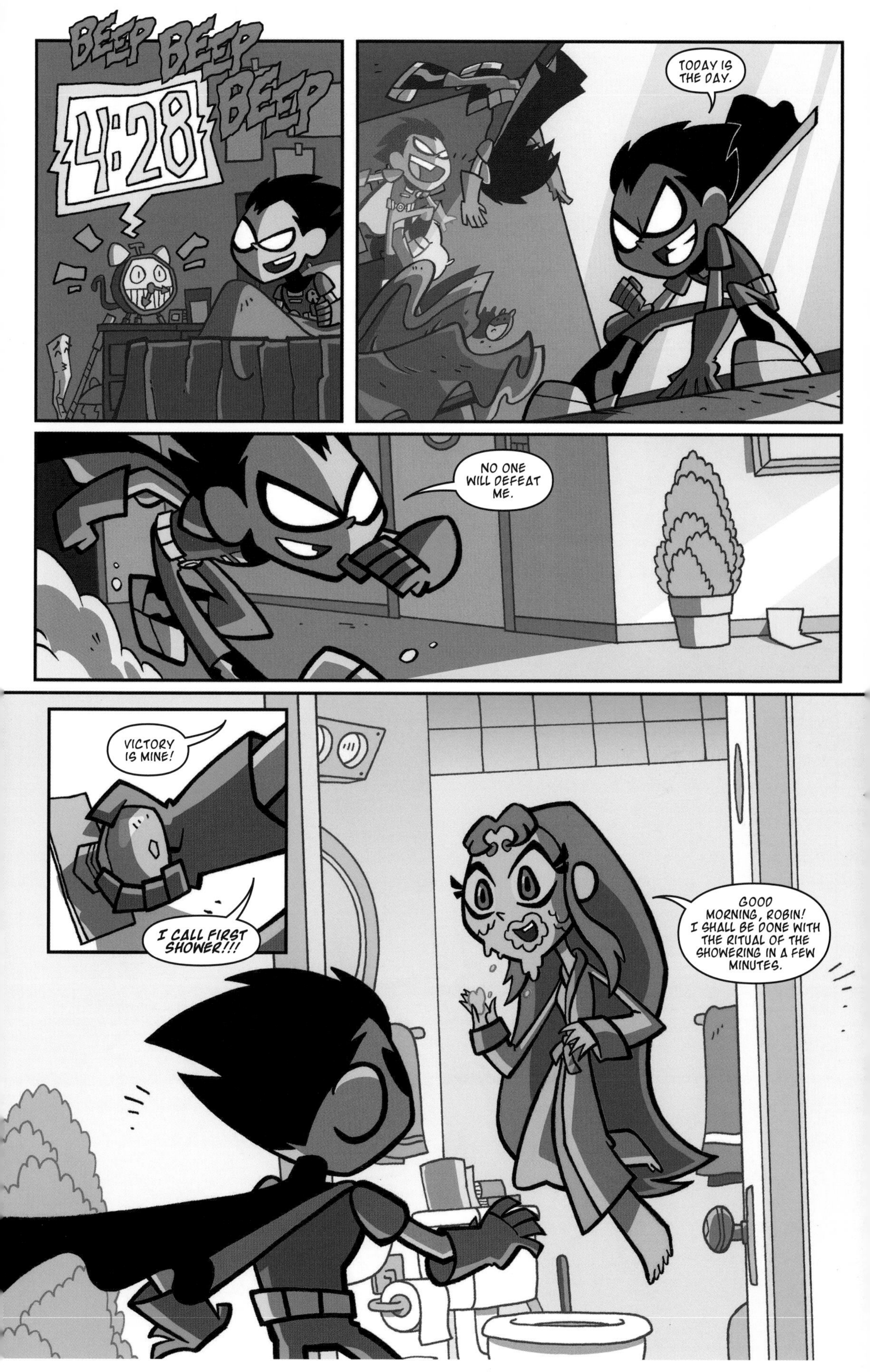

BEEP BEEP BEEP
4:28
TODAY IS THE DAY.
NO ONE WILL DEFEAT ME.
VICTORY IS MINE!
I CALL FIRST SHOWER!!!
GOOD MORNING, ROBIN! I SHALL BE DONE WITH THE RITUAL OF THE SHOWERING IN A FEW MINUTES.

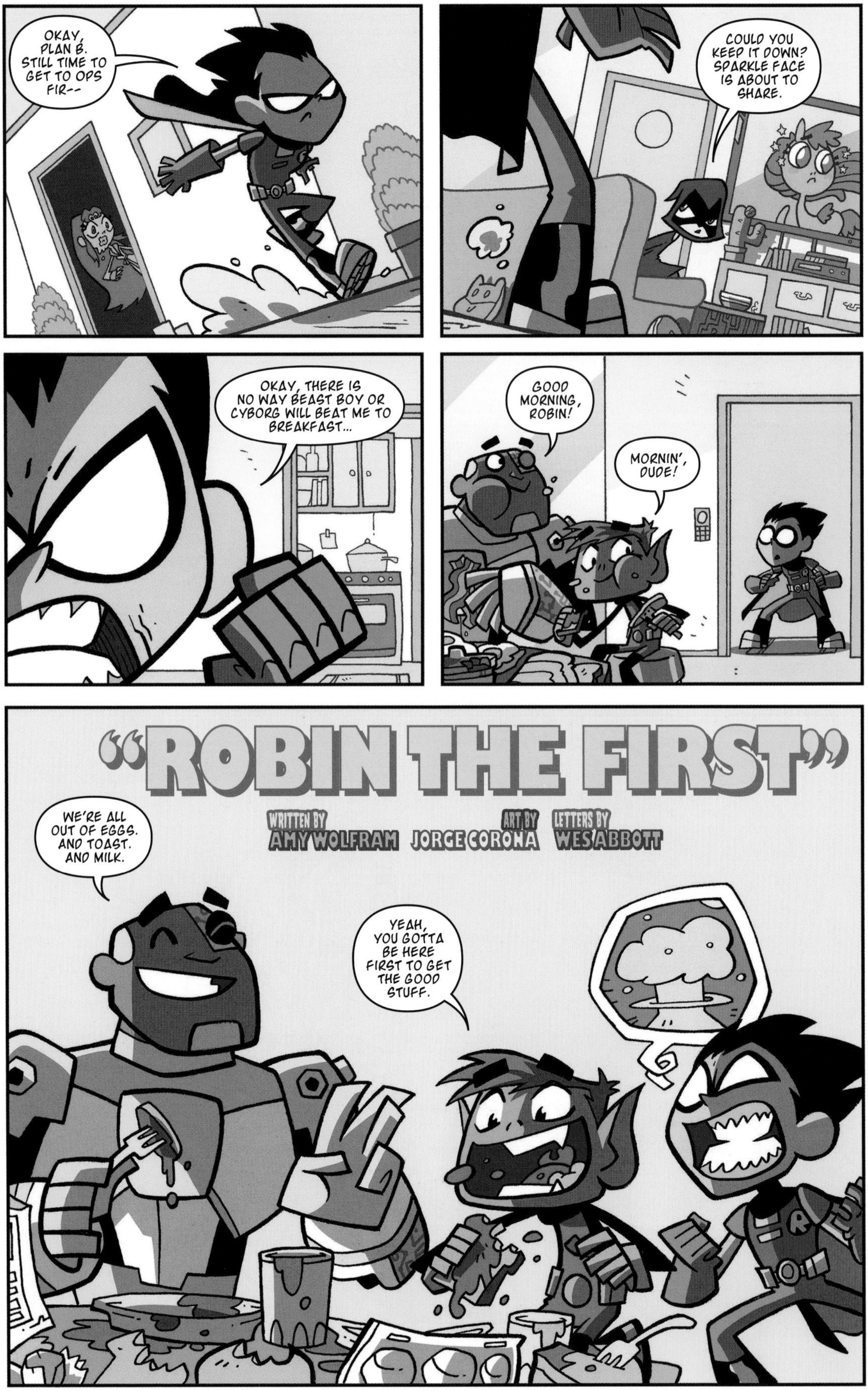
OKAY, PLAN B. STILL TIME TO GET TO OPS FIR--
COULD YOU KEEP IT DOWN? SPARKLE FACE IS ABOUT TO SHARE.
OKAY, THERE IS NO WAY BEAST BOY OR CYBORG WILL BEAT ME TO BREAKFAST...
GOOD MORNING, ROBIN!
MORNIN', DUDE!
"ROBIN THE FIRST"
WRITTEN BY AMY WOLFRAM
ART BY JORGE CORONA
LETTERS BY WES ABBOTT
WE'RE ALL OUT OF EGGS. AND TOAST. AND MILK.
YEAH, YOU GOTTA BE HERE FIRST TO GET THE GOOD STUFF.

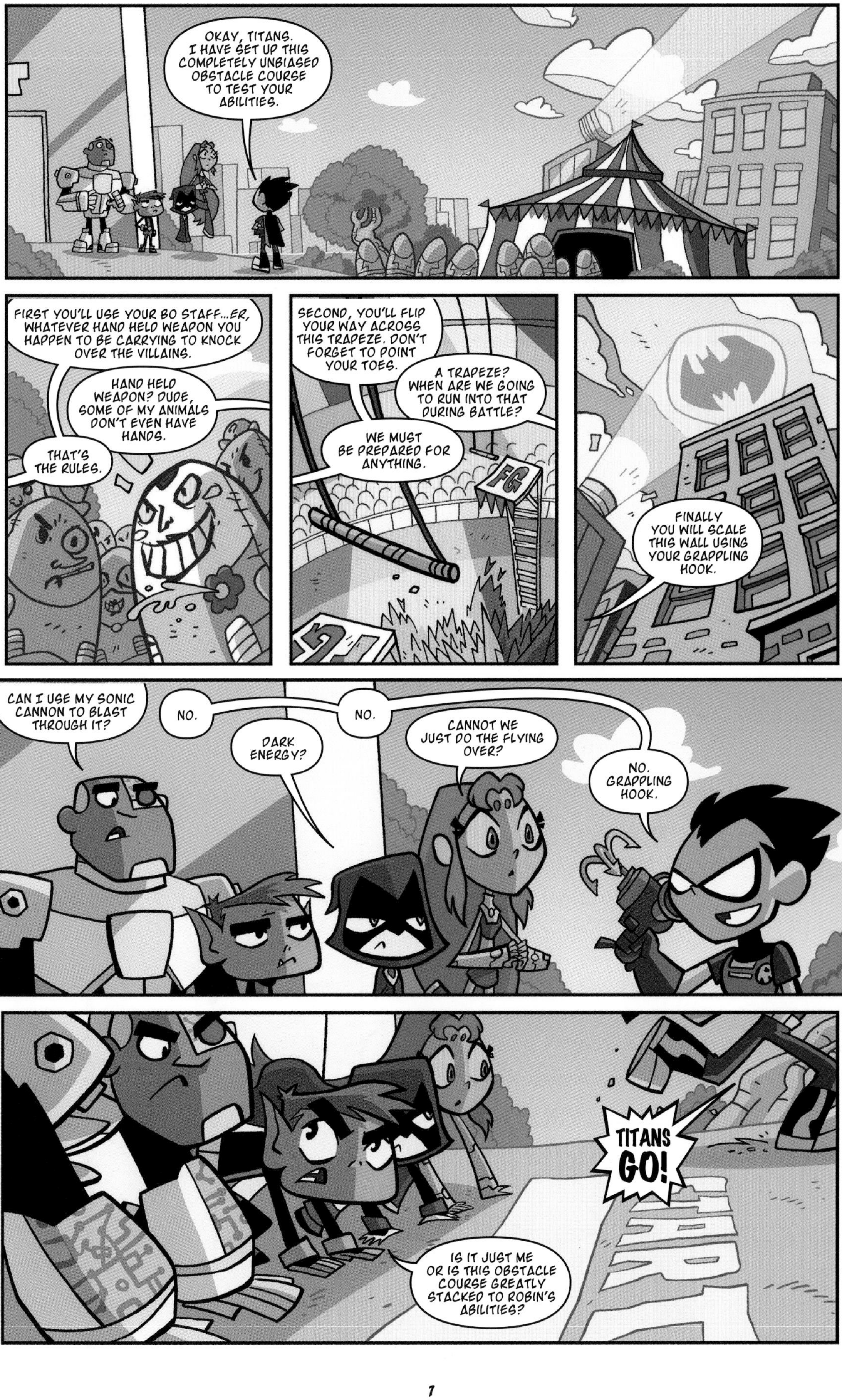

OKAY, TITANS. I HAVE SET UP THIS COMPLETELY UNBIASED OBSTACLE COURSE TO TEST YOUR ABILITIES.
FIRST YOU'LL USE YOUR BO STAFF...ER, WHATEVER HAND HELD WEAPON YOU HAPPEN TO BE CARRYING TO KNOCK OVER THE VILLAINS.
HAND HELD WEAPON? DUDE, SOME OF MY ANIMALS DON'T EVEN HAVE HANDS.
THAT'S THE RULES.
SECOND, YOU'LL FLIP YOUR WAY ACROSS THIS TRAPEZE. DON'T FORGET TO POINT YOUR TOES.
A TRAPEZE? WHEN ARE WE GOING TO RUN INTO THAT DURING BATTLE?
WE MUST BE PREPARED FOR ANYTHING.
FG
FINALLY YOU WILL SCALE THIS WALL USING YOUR GRAPPLING HOOK.
CAN I USE MY SONIC CANNON TO BLAST THROUGH IT?
NO.
DARK ENERGY?
NO.
CANNOT WE JUST DO THE FLYING OVER?
NO. GRAPPLING HOOK.
TITANS GO!
IS IT JUST ME OR IS THIS OBSTACLE COURSE GREATLY STACKED TO ROBIN'S ABILITIES?

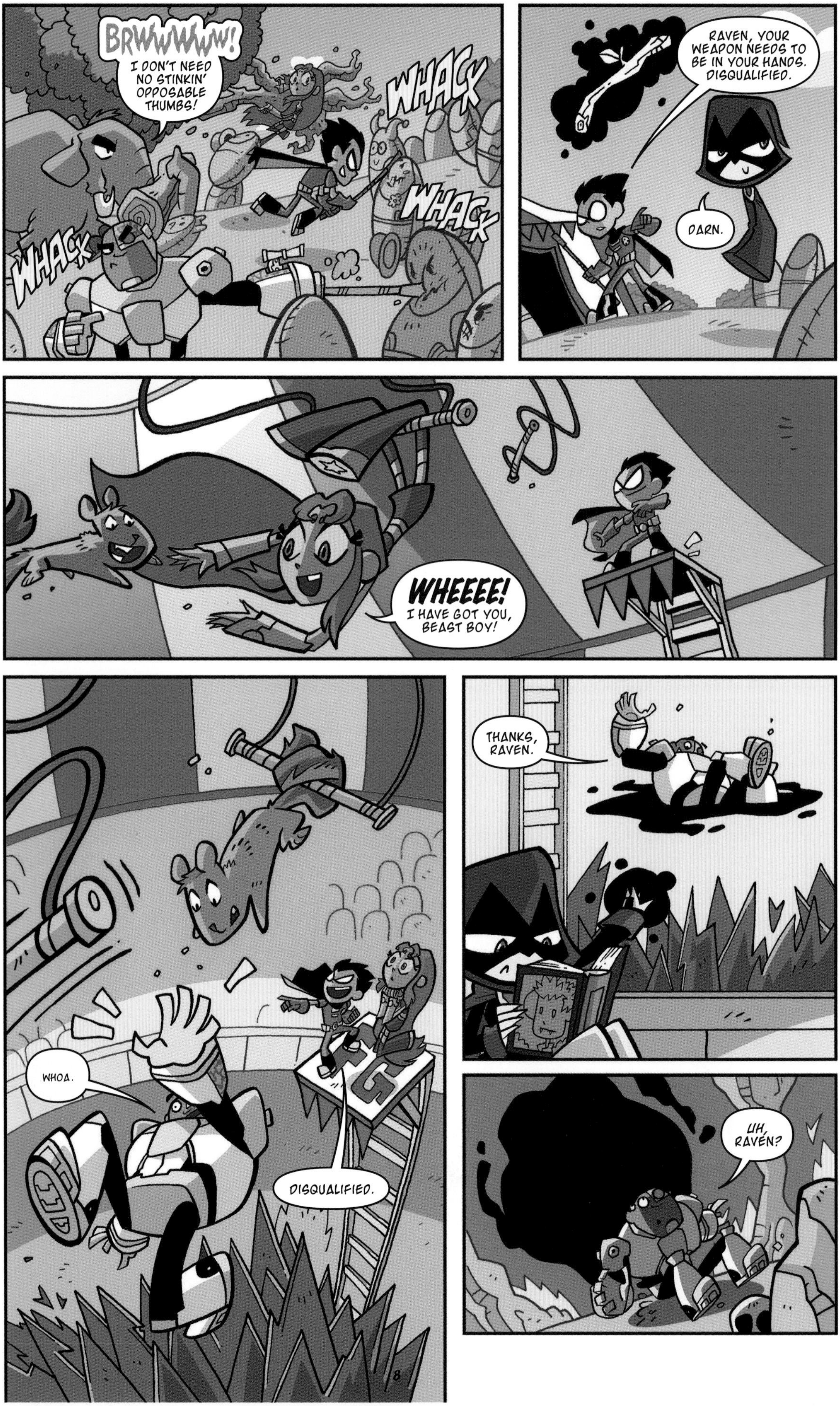
BRWWWWW!
I DON'T NEED NO STINKIN' OPPOSABLE THUMBS!
WHACK
WHACK
WHACK
RAVEN, YOUR WEAPON NEEDS TO BE IN YOUR HANDS. DISQUALIFIED.
DARN.
WHEEEE! I HAVE GOT YOU, BEAST BOY!
WHOA.
DISQUALIFIED.
THANKS, RAVEN.
UH, RAVEN?

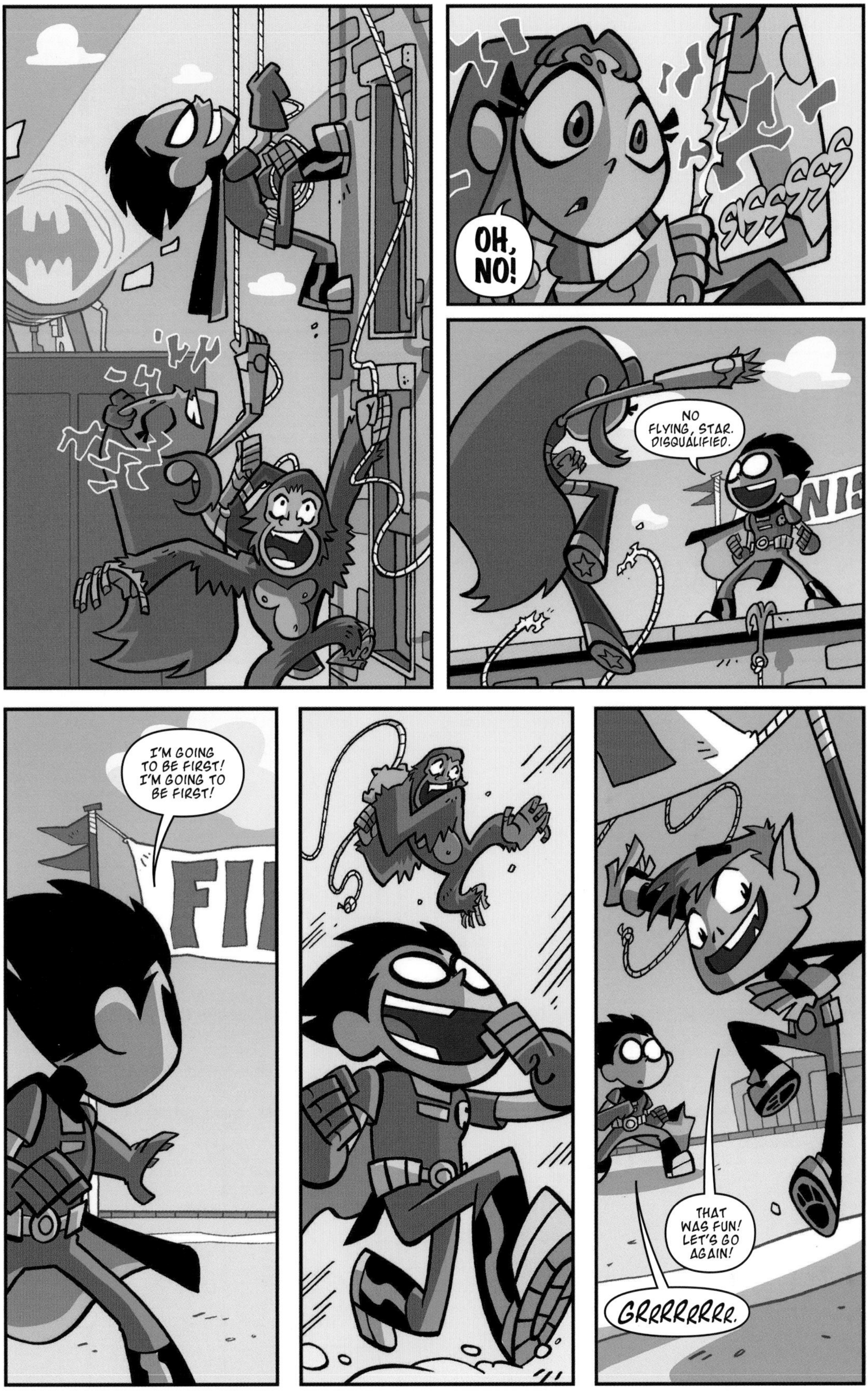
OH, NO!
SISSSSS
NO FLYING, STAR. DISQUALIFIED.
I'M GOING TO BE FIRST! I'M GOING TO BE FIRST!
THAT WAS FUN! LET'S GO AGAIN!
GRRRRRRRR.

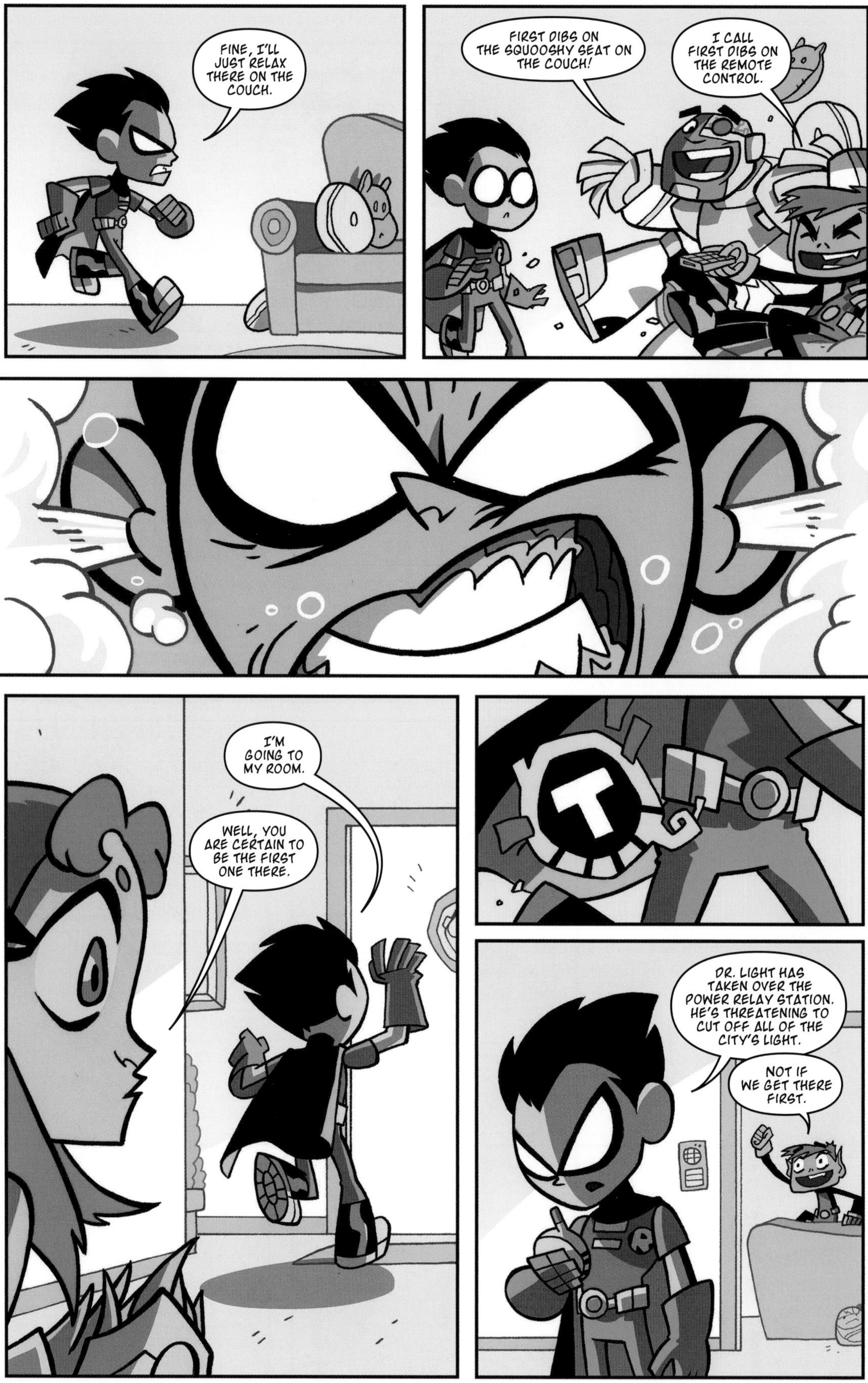
FINE, I'LL JUST RELAX THERE ON THE COUCH.
FIRST DIBS ON THE SQUOOSHY SEAT ON THE COUCH!
I CALL FIRST DIBS ON THE REMOTE CONTROL.
I'M GOING TO MY ROOM.
WELL, YOU ARE CERTAIN TO BE THE FIRST ONE THERE.
DR. LIGHT HAS TAKEN OVER THE POWER RELAY STATION. HE'S THREATENING TO CUT OFF ALL OF THE CITY'S LIGHT.
NOT IF WE GET THERE FIRST.

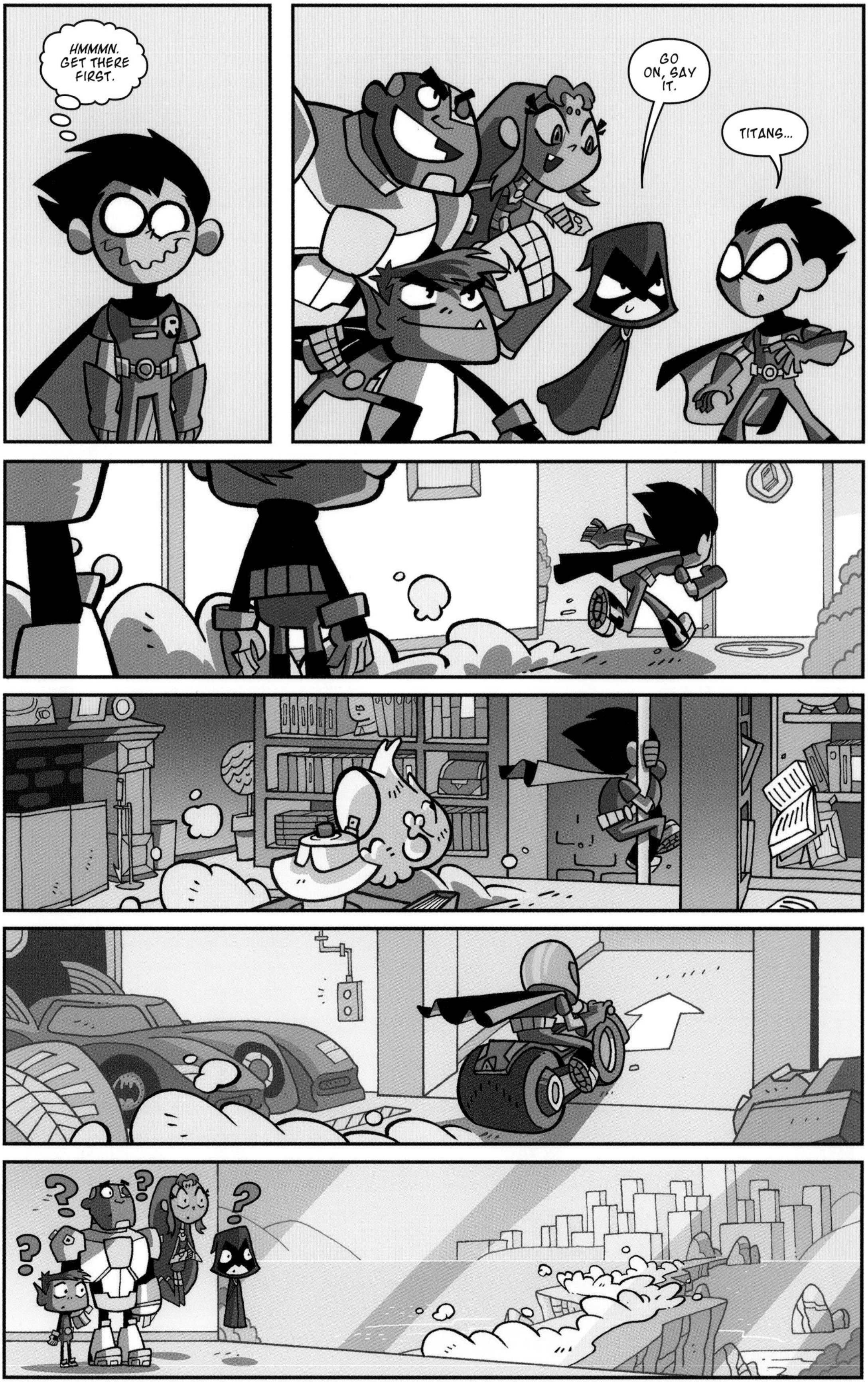
HMMMN. GET THERE FIRST.
GO ON, SAY IT.
TITANS...

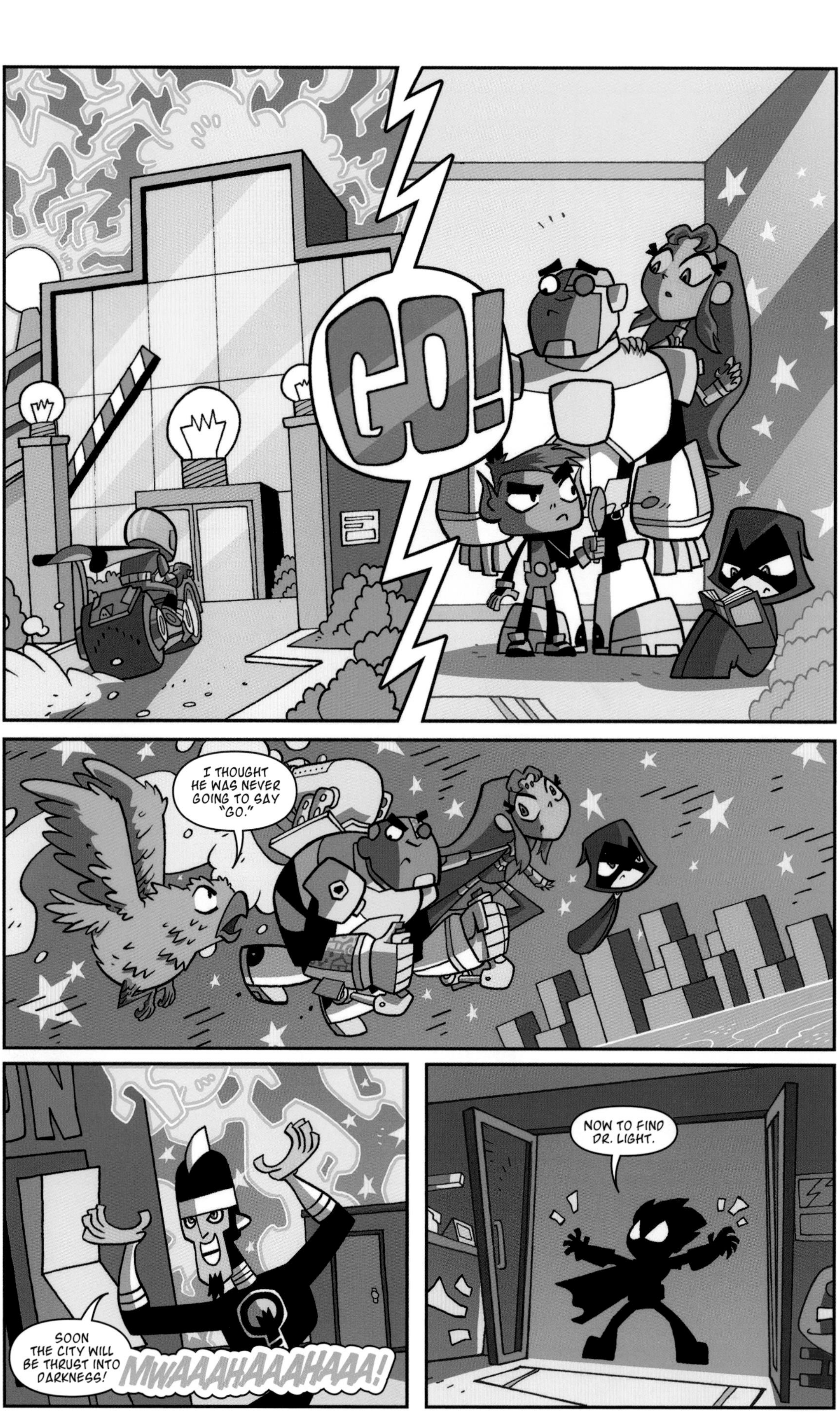
GO!
I THOUGHT HE WAS NEVER GOING TO SAY "GO."
SOON THE CITY WILL BE THRUST INTO DARKNESS!
MWAAAHAAAHAAA!
NOW TO FIND DR. LIGHT.

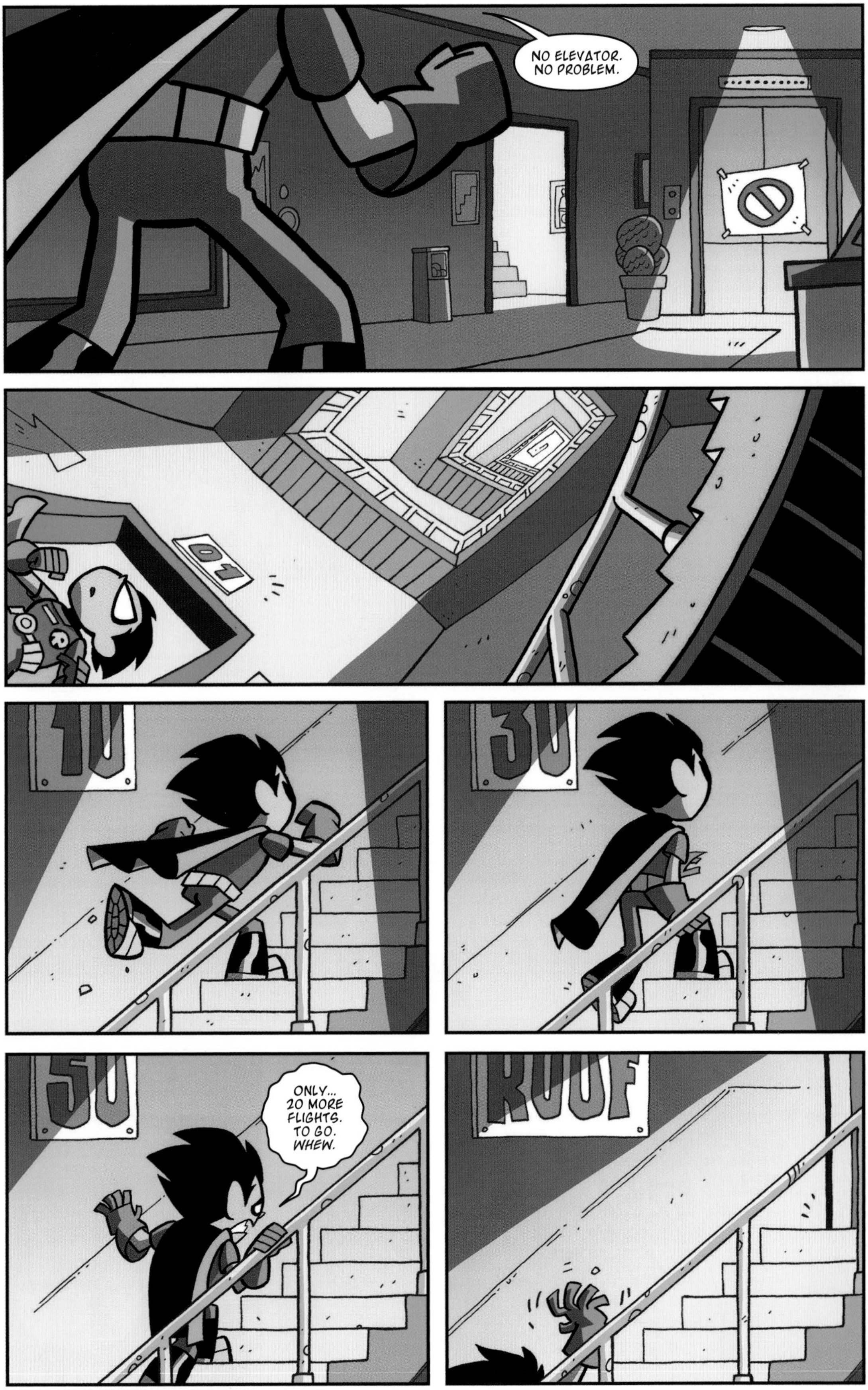
NO ELEVATOR. NO PROBLEM.
10
30
50
ONLY... 20 MORE FLIGHTS. TO GO. WHEW.
ROOF

WELL, ROBIN, LOOKS LIKE YOU'RE THE FIRST TO ARRIVE.

YES! FIRST!

AND NOW YOU'LL BE THE FIRST TO SEE JUMP CITY EXPERIENCE THE ULTIMATE LIGHTS OUT!

YOU... WON'T... GET... AWAY... WITH...

HOLD ON... JUST ONE... SECOND...WHILE I CATCH MY... BREATH.

UGHHHHHH.

IT'S NO FUN IF YOU'RE NOT GOING TO FIGHT.

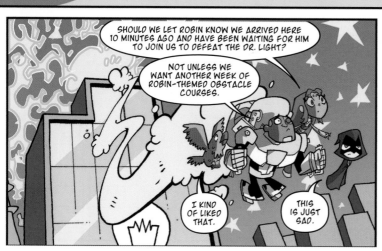

SHOULD WE LET ROBIN KNOW WE ARRIVED HERE 10 MINUTES AGO AND HAVE BEEN WAITING FOR HIM TO JOIN US TO DEFEAT THE DR. LIGHT?

NOT UNLESS WE WANT ANOTHER WEEK OF ROBIN-THEMED OBSTACLE COURSES.

I KIND OF LIKED THAT.

THIS IS JUST SAD.

I'M COMING... JUST A SECOND... UGGGHHHH.

ALL RIGHT. THAT'S IT, I'M JUST GOING TO FLIP IT OFF. IN 5, 4, 3, 2...

THE END

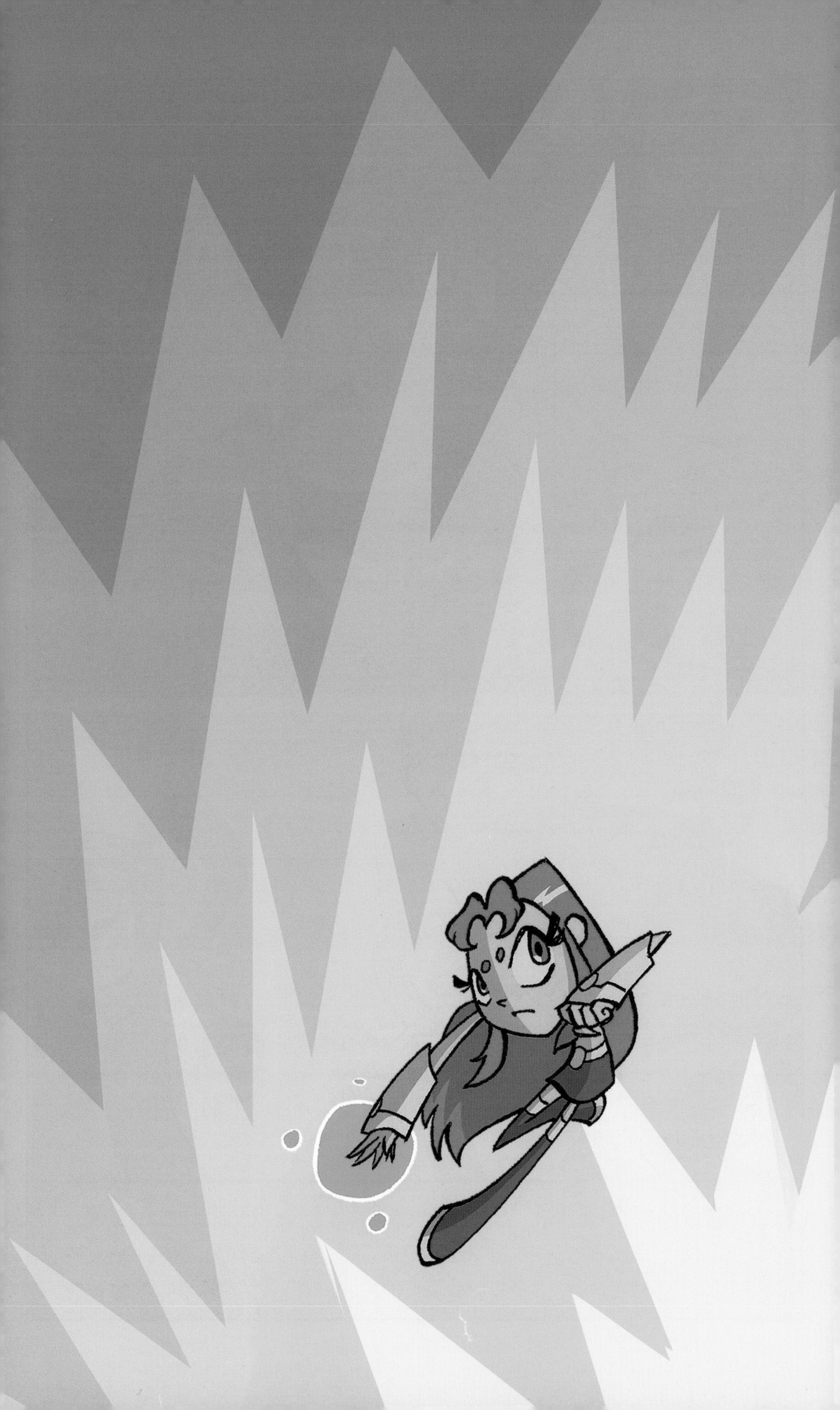

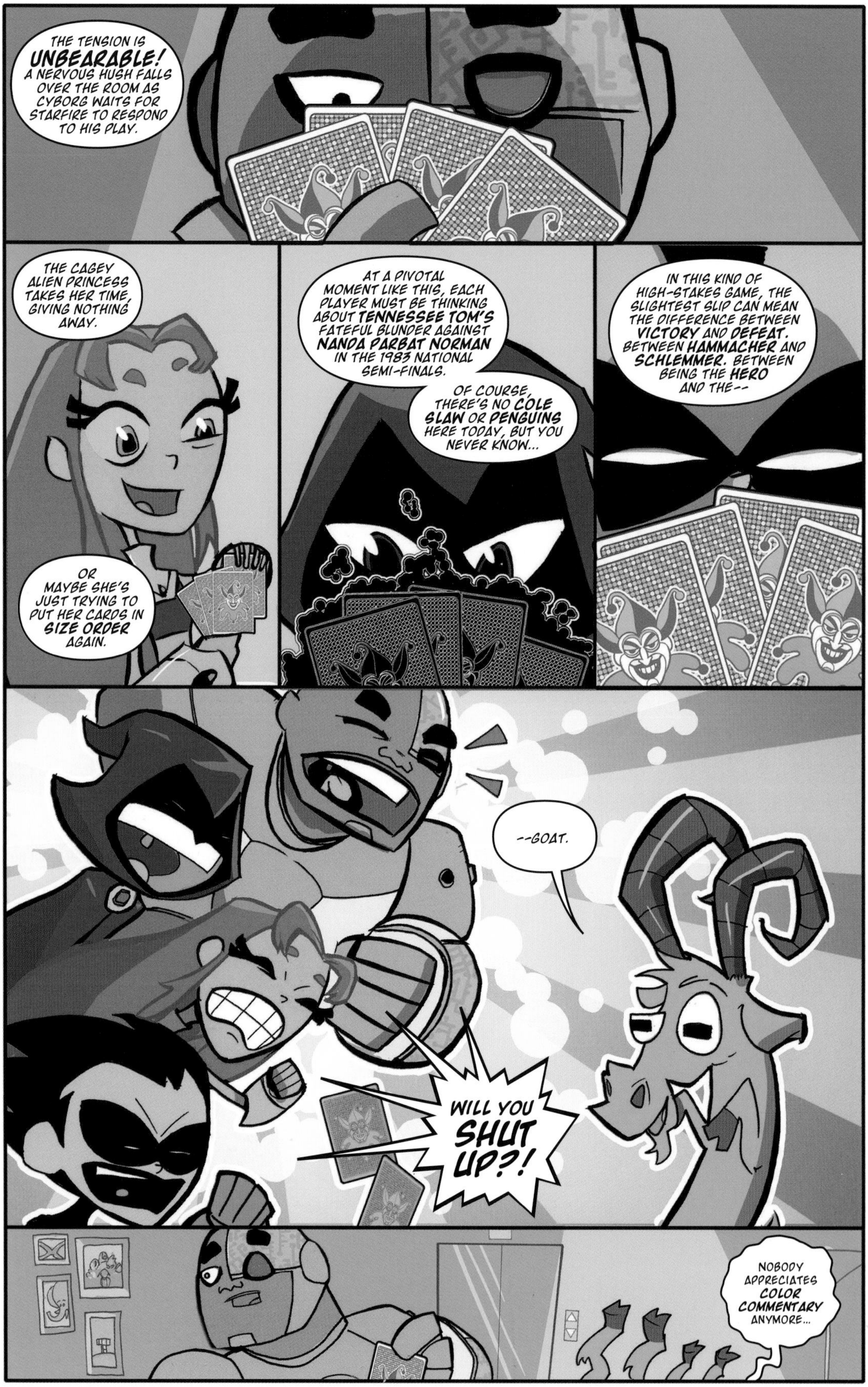
THE TENSION IS UNBEARABLE! A NERVOUS HUSH FALLS OVER THE ROOM AS CYBORG WAITS FOR STARFIRE TO RESPOND TO HIS PLAY.
THE CAGEY ALIEN PRINCESS TAKES HER TIME, GIVING NOTHING AWAY.
OR MAYBE SHE'S JUST TRYING TO PUT HER CARDS IN SIZE ORDER AGAIN.
AT A PIVOTAL MOMENT LIKE THIS, EACH PLAYER MUST BE THINKING ABOUT TENNESSEE TOM'S FATEFUL BLUNDER AGAINST NANDA PARBAT NORMAN IN THE 1983 NATIONAL SEMI-FINALS.
OF COURSE, THERE'S NO COLE SLAW OR PENGUINS HERE TODAY, BUT YOU NEVER KNOW...
IN THIS KIND OF HIGH-STAKES GAME, THE SLIGHTEST SLIP CAN MEAN THE DIFFERENCE BETWEEN VICTORY AND DEFEAT. BETWEEN HAMMACHER AND SCHLEMMER. BETWEEN BEING THE HERO AND THE--
--GOAT.
WILL YOU SHUT UP?!
NOBODY APPRECIATES COLOR COMMENTARY ANYMORE...

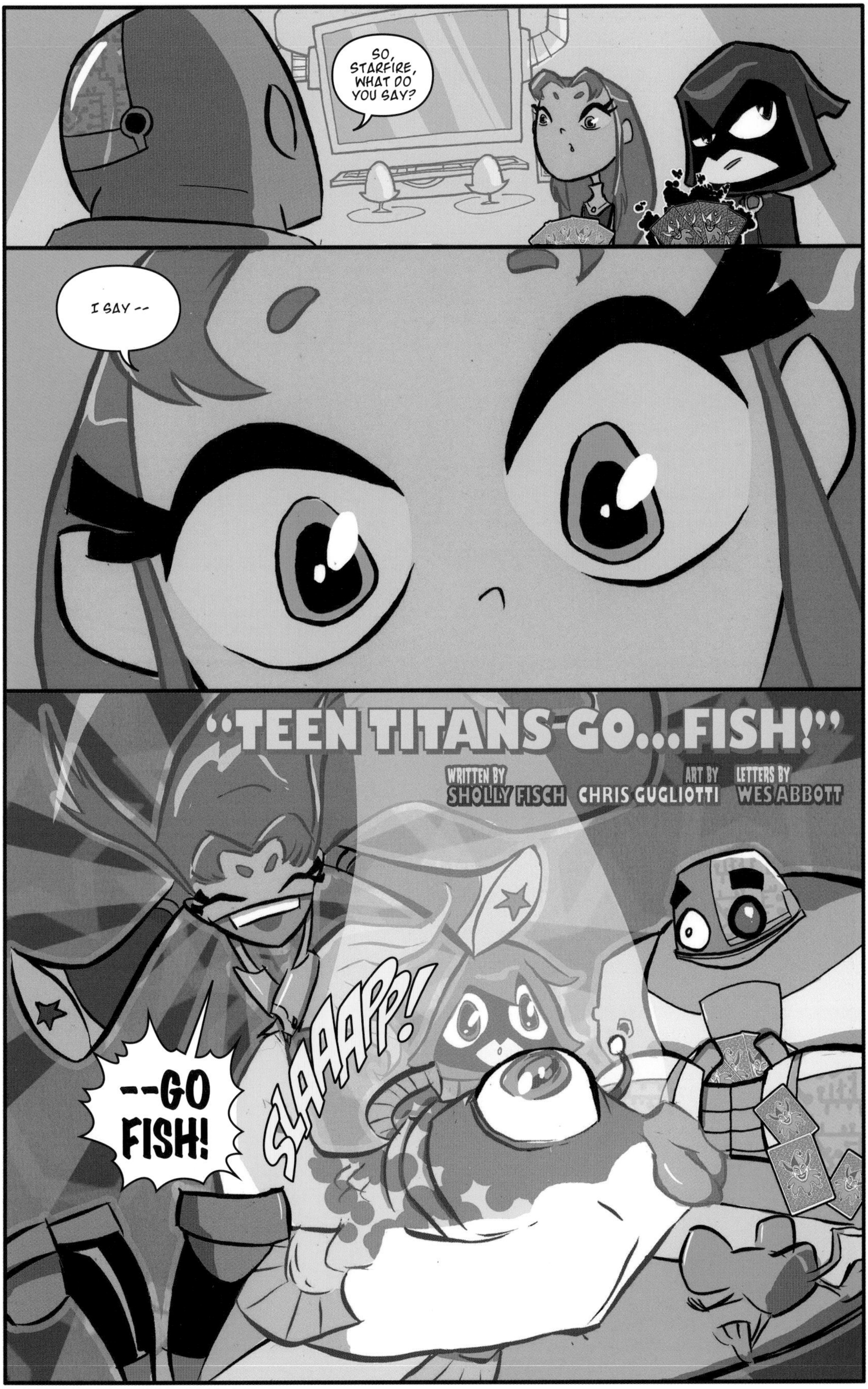
SO, STARFIRE, WHAT DO YOU SAY?
I SAY --
"TEEN TITANS GO...FISH!"
WRITTEN BY SHOLLY FISCH
ART BY CHRIS GUGLIOTTI
LETTERS BY WES ABBOTT
--GO FISH!
SLAAAPP!

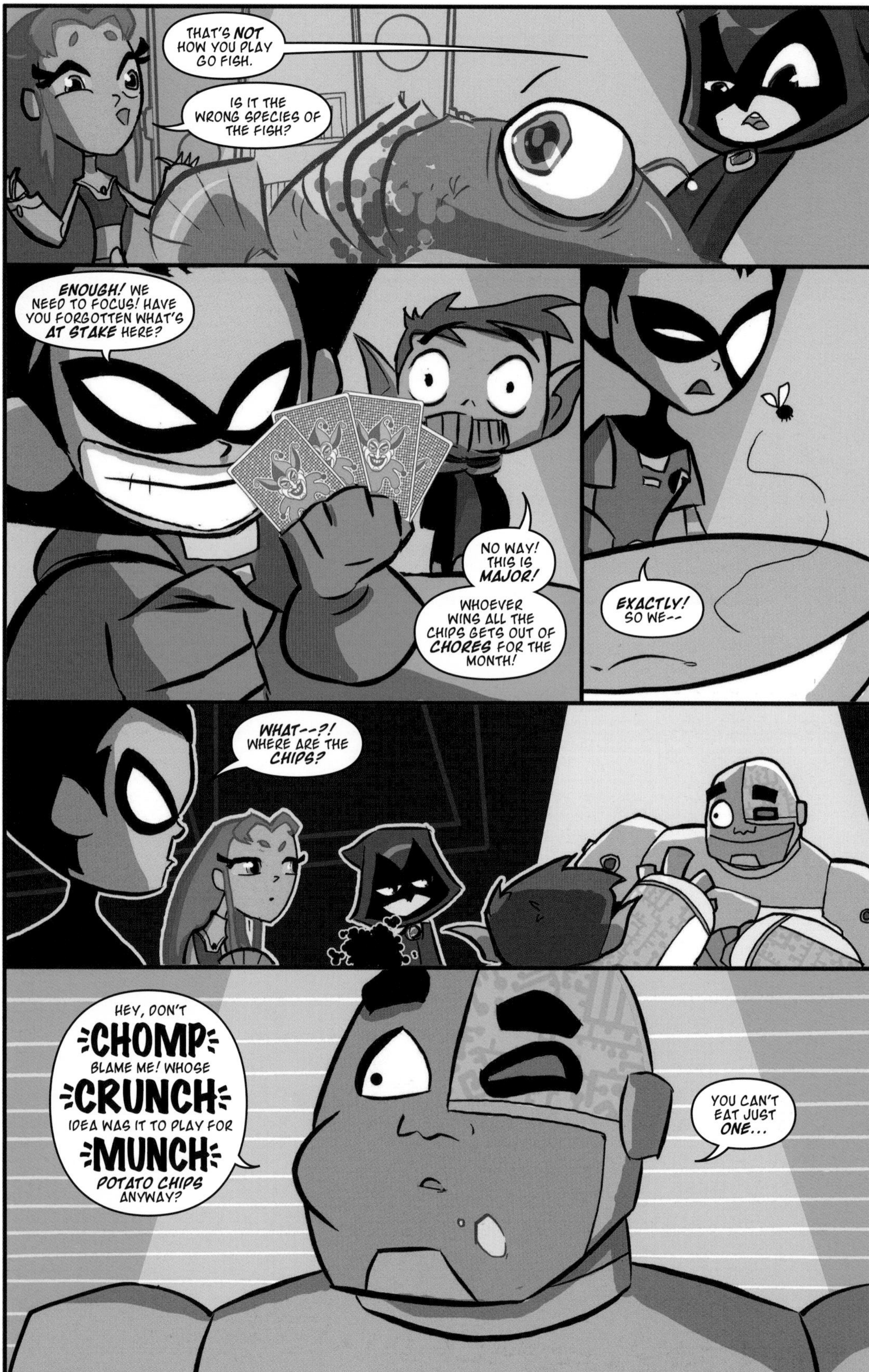
THAT'S NOT HOW YOU PLAY GO FISH.
IS IT THE WRONG SPECIES OF THE FISH?
ENOUGH! WE NEED TO FOCUS! HAVE YOU FORGOTTEN WHAT'S AT STAKE HERE?
NO WAY! THIS IS MAJOR!
WHOEVER WINS ALL THE CHIPS GETS OUT OF CHORES FOR THE MONTH!
EXACTLY! SO WE--
WHAT--?! WHERE ARE THE CHIPS?
HEY, DON'T CHOMP BLAME ME! WHOSE CRUNCH IDEA WAS IT TO PLAY FOR MUNCH POTATO CHIPS ANYWAY?
YOU CAN'T EAT JUST ONE...

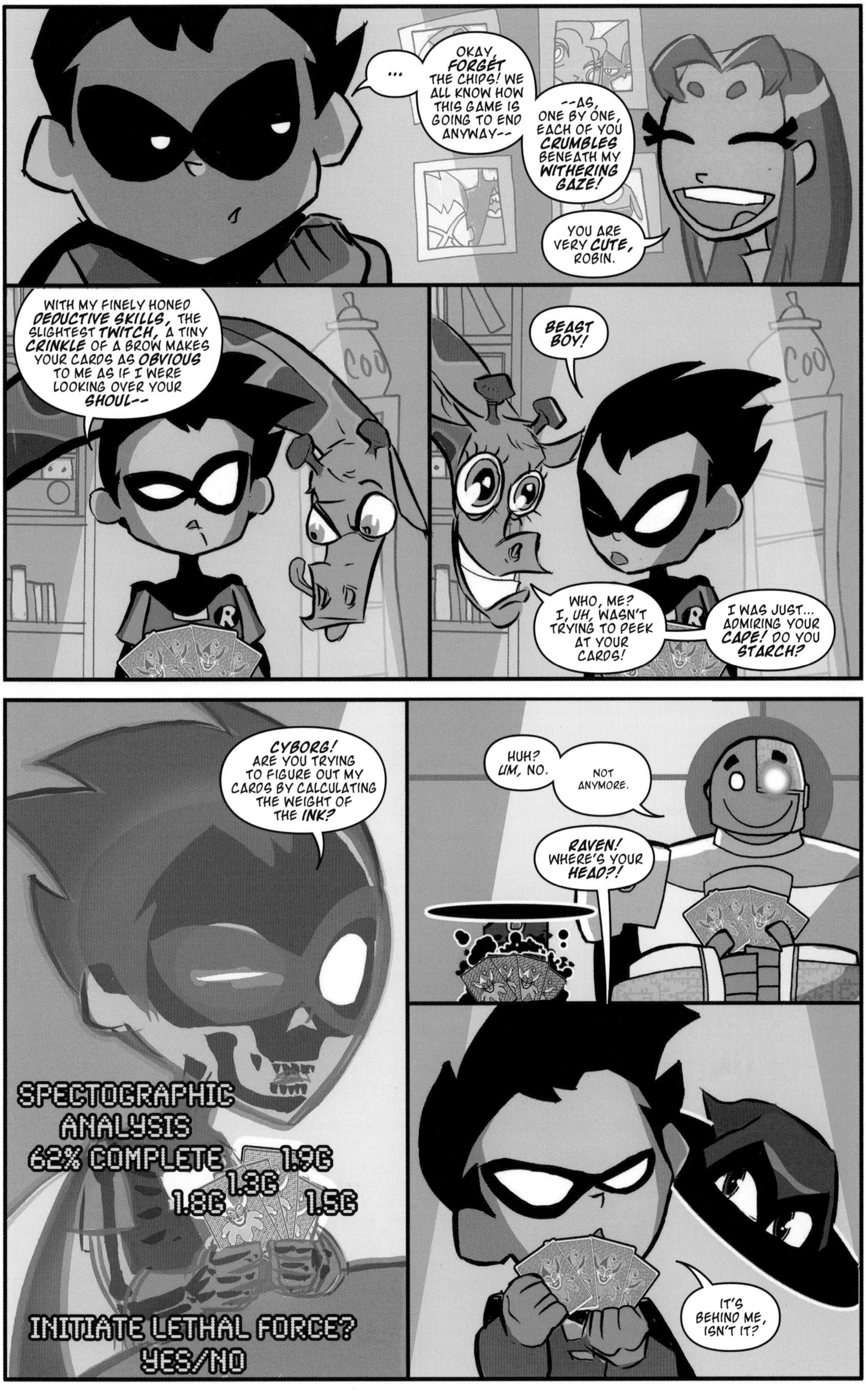
...
OKAY, FORGET THE CHIPS! WE ALL KNOW HOW THIS GAME IS GOING TO END ANYWAY--
--AS, ONE BY ONE, EACH OF YOU CRUMBLES BENEATH MY WITHERING GAZE!
YOU ARE VERY CUTE, ROBIN.
WITH MY FINELY HONED DEDUCTIVE SKILLS, THE SLIGHTEST TWITCH, A TINY CRINKLE OF A BROW MAKES YOUR CARDS AS OBVIOUS TO ME AS IF I WERE LOOKING OVER YOUR SHOUL--
BEAST BOY!
WHO, ME? I, UH, WASN'T TRYING TO PEEK AT YOUR CARDS!
I WAS JUST... ADMIRING YOUR CAPE! DO YOU STARCH?
CYBORG! ARE YOU TRYING TO FIGURE OUT MY CARDS BY CALCULATING THE WEIGHT OF THE INK?
SPECTOGRAPHIC ANALYSIS 62% COMPLETE
1.9G
1.3G
1.8G
1.5G
INITIATE LETHAL FORCE? YES/NO
HUH? UM, NO.
NOT ANYMORE.
RAVEN! WHERE'S YOUR HEAD?!
IT'S BEHIND ME, ISN'T IT?

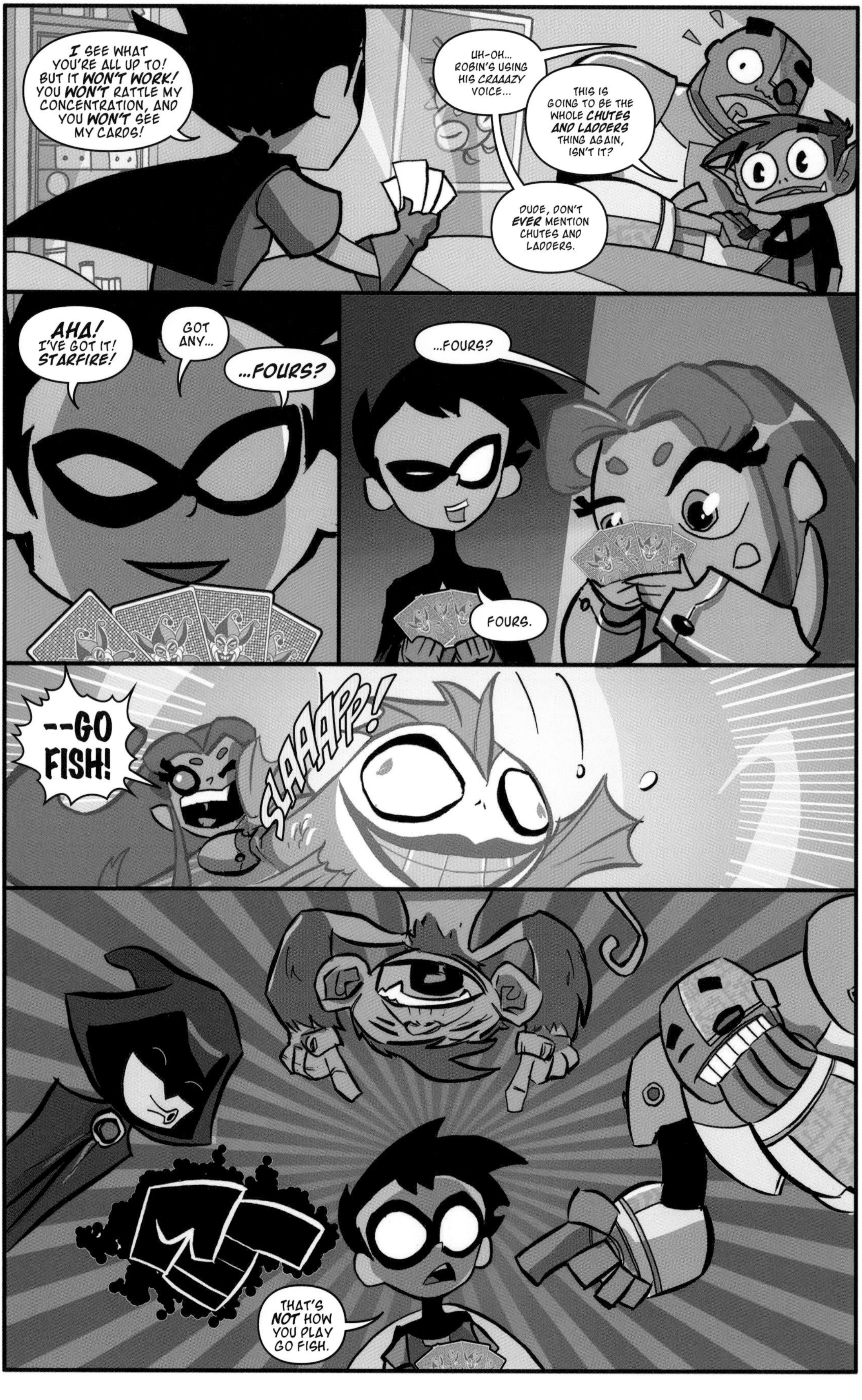
I SEE WHAT YOU'RE ALL UP TO! BUT IT WON'T WORK! YOU WON'T RATTLE MY CONCENTRATION, AND YOU WON'T SEE MY CARDS!
UH-OH... ROBIN'S USING HIS CRAAAZY VOICE...
THIS IS GOING TO BE THE WHOLE CHUTES AND LADDERS THING AGAIN, ISN'T IT?
DUDE, DON'T EVER MENTION CHUTES AND LADDERS.
AHA! I'VE GOT IT! STARFIRE!
GOT ANY...
...FOURS?
...FOURS?
FOURS.
--GO FISH!
SLAAAPP!
THAT'S NOT HOW YOU PLAY GO FISH.

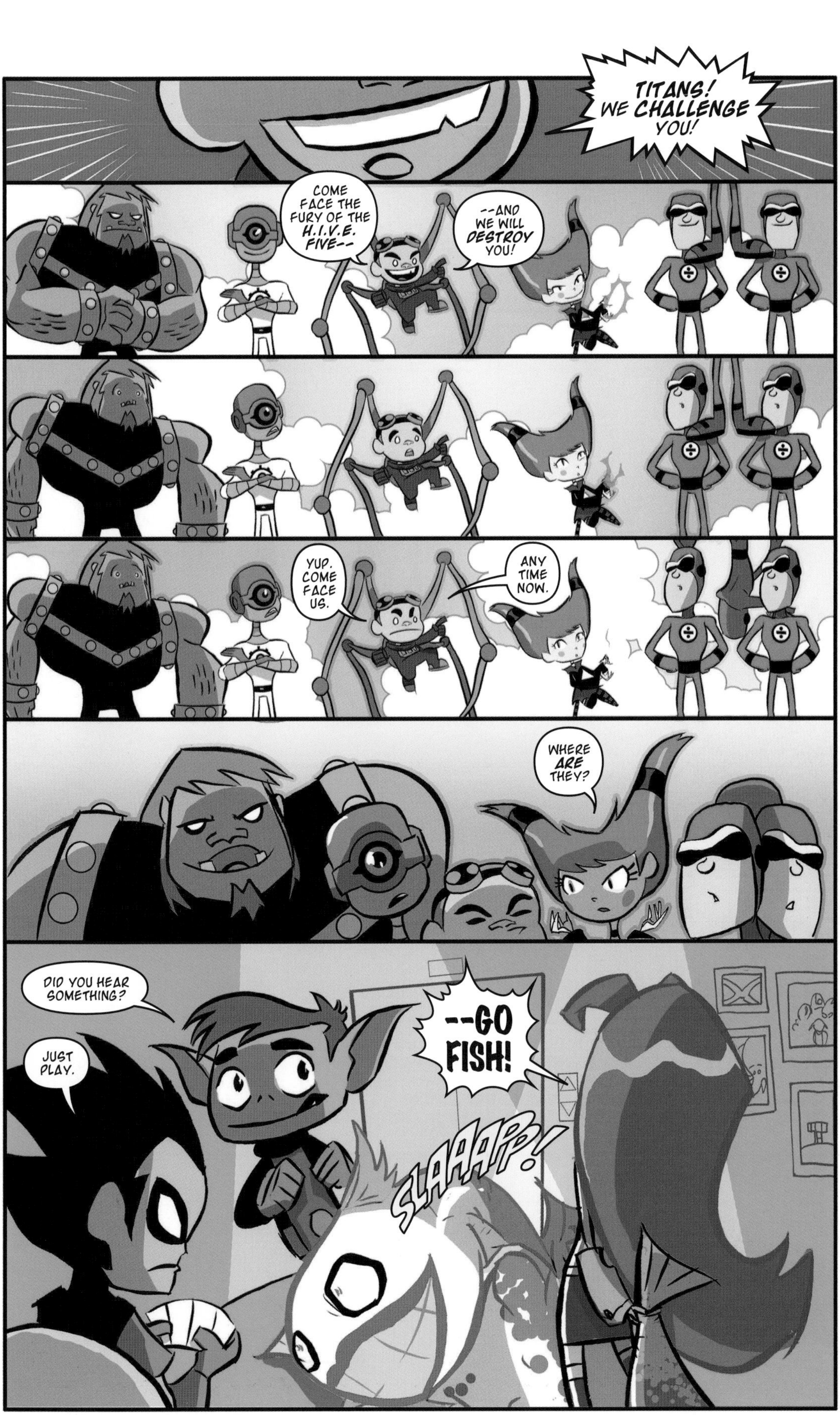
TITANS! WE CHALLENGE YOU!
COME FACE THE FURY OF THE H.I.V.E. FIVE--
--AND WE WILL DESTROY YOU!
YUP. COME FACE US.
ANY TIME NOW.
WHERE ARE THEY?
DID YOU HEAR SOMETHING?
JUST PLAY.
--GO FISH!
SLAAAP!

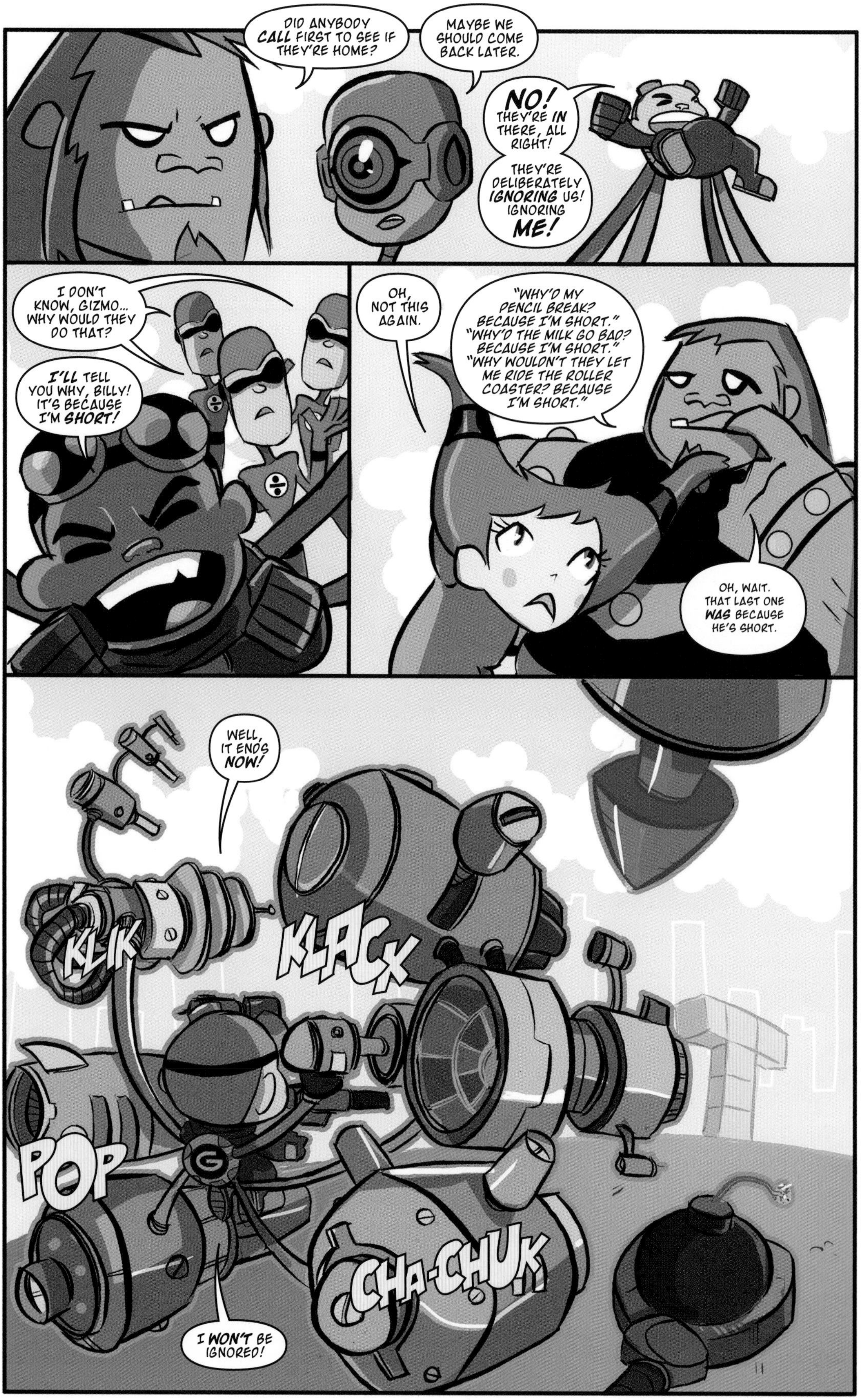
DID ANYBODY CALL FIRST TO SEE IF THEY'RE HOME?
MAYBE WE SHOULD COME BACK LATER.
NO! THEY'RE IN THERE, ALL RIGHT!
THEY'RE DELIBERATELY IGNORING US! IGNORING ME!
I DON'T KNOW, GIZMO... WHY WOULD THEY DO THAT?
I'LL TELL YOU WHY, BILLY! IT'S BECAUSE I'M SHORT!
OH, NOT THIS AGAIN.
"WHY'D MY PENCIL BREAK? BECAUSE I'M SHORT." "WHY'D THE MILK GO BAD? BECAUSE I'M SHORT." "WHY WOULDN'T THEY LET ME RIDE THE ROLLER COASTER? BECAUSE I'M SHORT."
OH, WAIT. THAT LAST ONE WAS BECAUSE HE'S SHORT.
WELL, IT ENDS NOW!
KLIK
KLACK
POP
CHA-CHUK
I WON'T BE IGNORED!

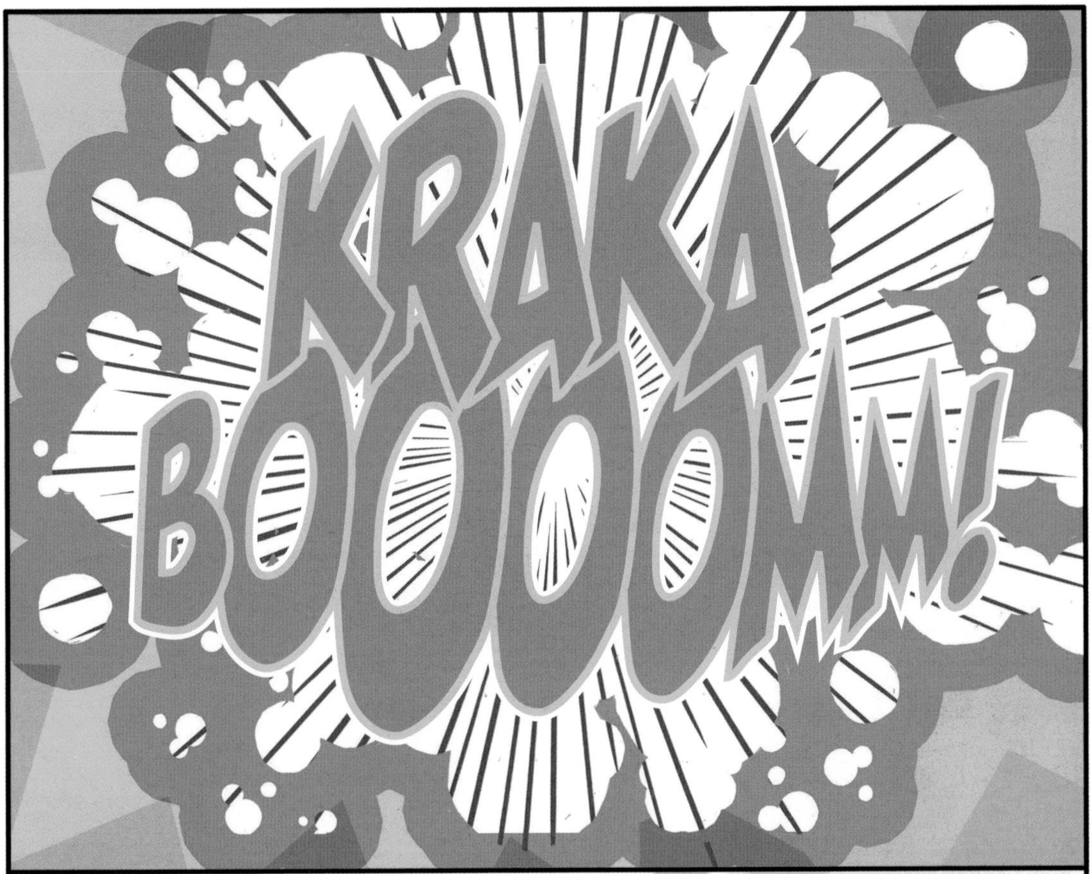
KRAKA BOOOOMMM!

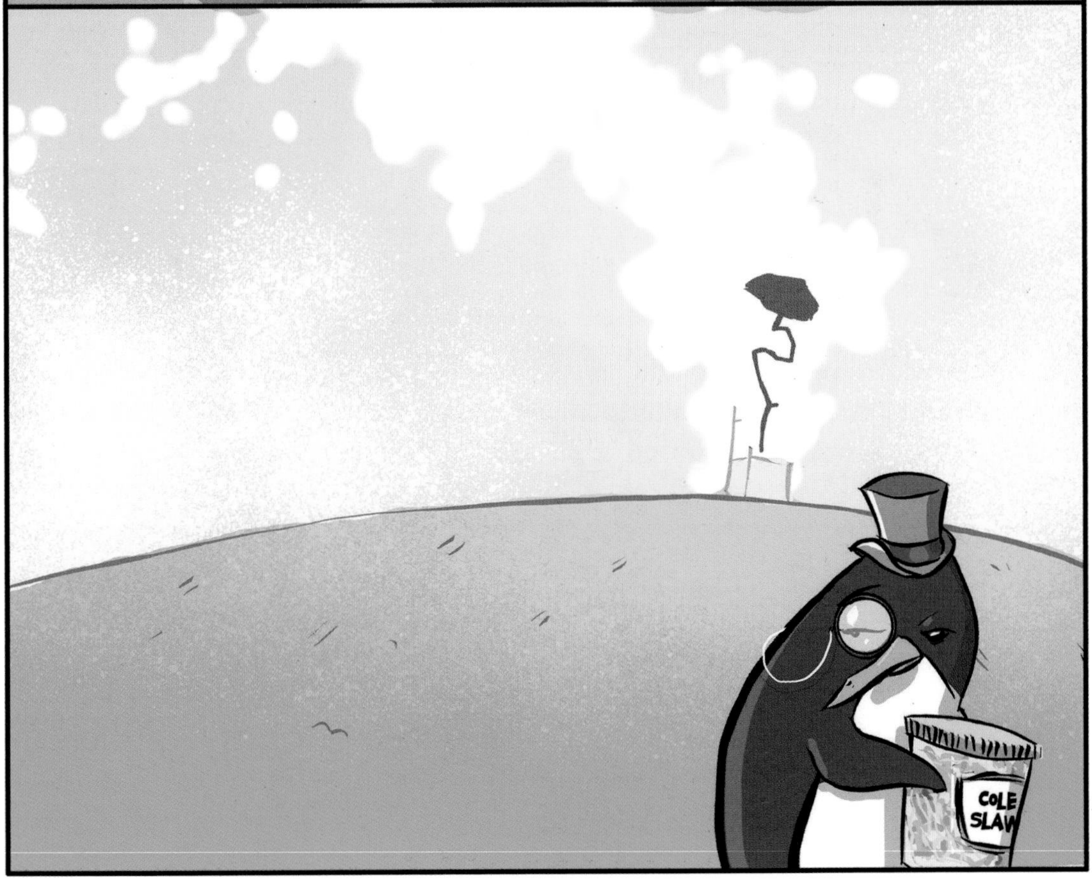
COLE SLAW

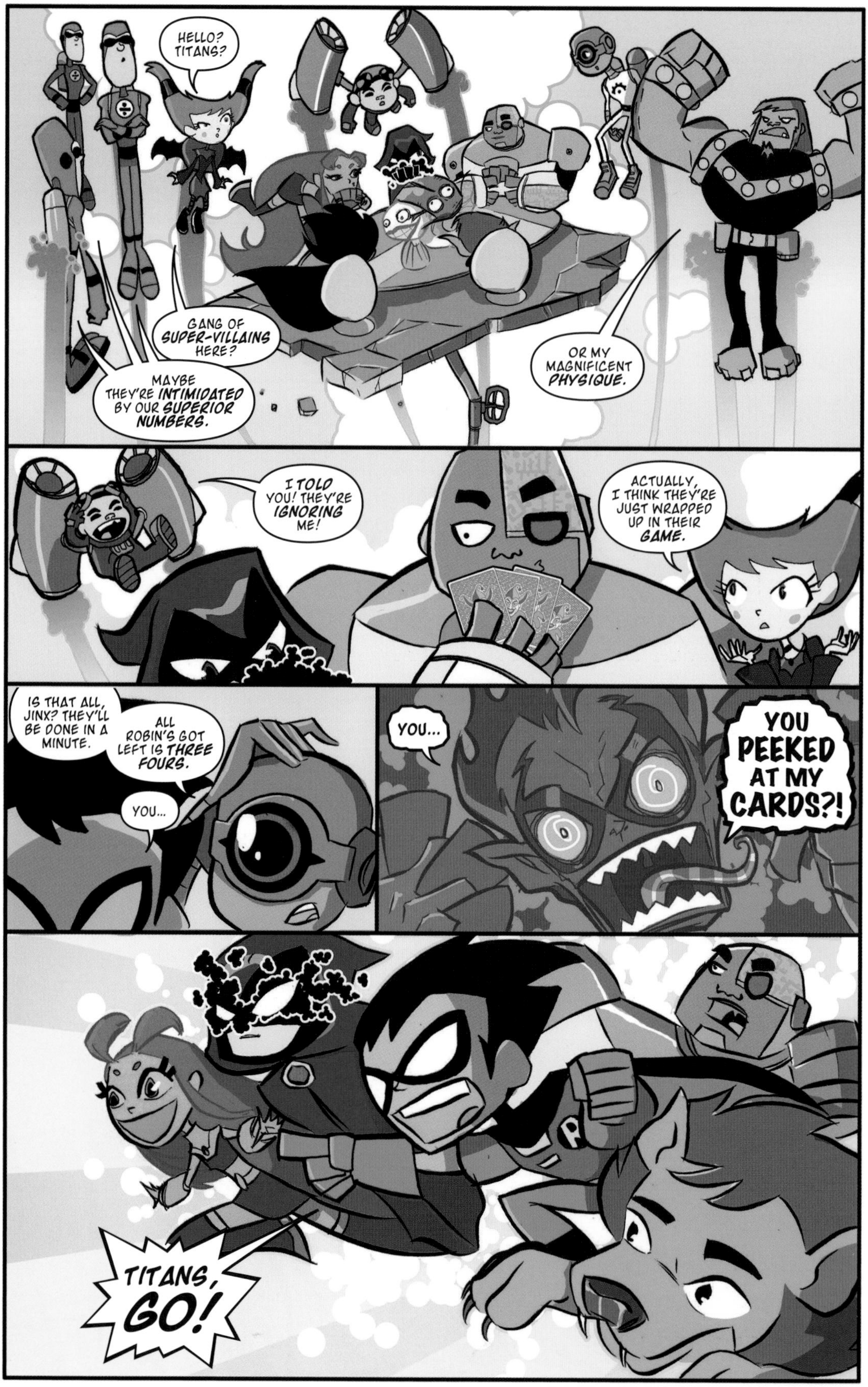
HELLO? TITANS?
GANG OF SUPER-VILLAINS HERE?
MAYBE THEY'RE INTIMIDATED BY OUR SUPERIOR NUMBERS.
OR MY MAGNIFICENT PHYSIQUE.
I TOLD YOU! THEY'RE IGNORING ME!
ACTUALLY, I THINK THEY'RE JUST WRAPPED UP IN THEIR GAME.
IS THAT ALL, JINX? THEY'LL BE DONE IN A MINUTE.
ALL ROBIN'S GOT LEFT IS THREE FOURS.
YOU...
YOU...
YOU PEEKED AT MY CARDS?!
TITANS, GO!

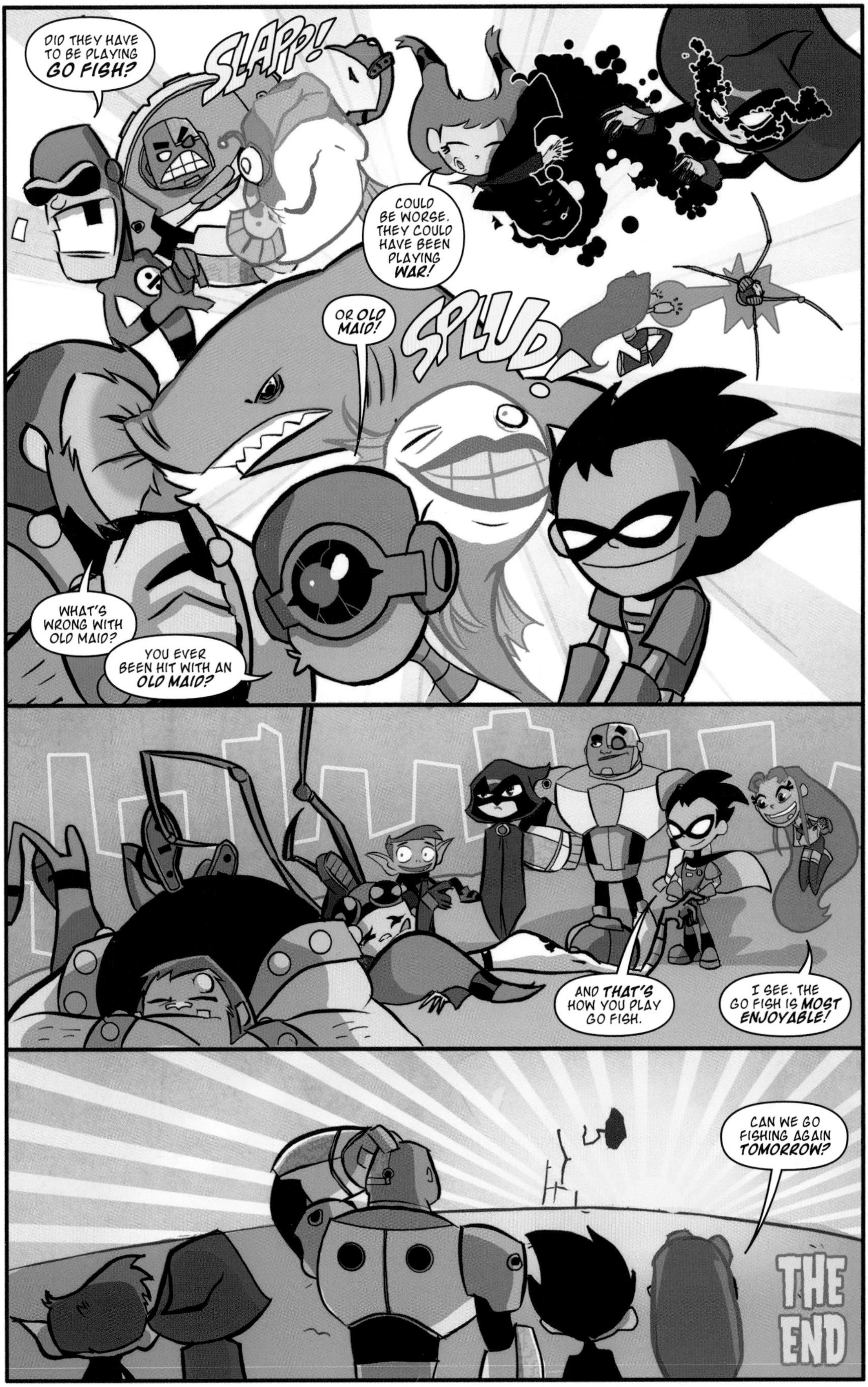
DID THEY HAVE TO BE PLAYING GO FISH?
SLAPP!
COULD BE WORSE. THEY COULD HAVE BEEN PLAYING WAR!
OR OLD MAID!
SPLUD!
WHAT'S WRONG WITH OLD MAID?
YOU EVER BEEN HIT WITH AN OLD MAID?
AND THAT'S HOW YOU PLAY GO FISH.
I SEE. THE GO FISH IS MOST ENJOYABLE!
CAN WE GO FISHING AGAIN TOMORROW?
THE END

CREATORS

AMY WOLFRAM

Amy Wolfram is a comic book and television writer. She has written episodes for the animated TV series *Teen Titans*, *Legion of Super-Heroes*, and *Teen Titans Go!*. In addition to the *Teen Titans Go!* comic book series, she has also written for *Teen Titans: Year One*.

SHOLLY FISCH

Bitten by a radioactive typewriter, Sholly Fisch has spent the wee hours writing books, comics, TV scripts, and online material for over 25 years. His comic book credits include more than 200 stories and features about characters such as Batman, Superman, Bugs Bunny, Daffy Duck, Spider-Man, and Ben 10. Currently, he writes stories for Action Comics every month, plus stories for Looney Tunes and Scooby-Doo. By day, Sholly is a mild-mannered developmental psychologist who helps to create educational TV shows, web sites, and other media for kids.

JORGE CORONA

Jorge Corona is a Venezuelan comic artist who is well-known for his all-ages fantasy-adventure series *Feathers* and his work on *Jim Henson's The Storyteller: Dragons*. In addition to *Teen Titans Go!*, he has also worked on *Batman Beyond*, *Justice League Beyond*, *We Are Robin*, *Goners*, and many other comics.

CHRIS GUGLIOTTI

Chris Gugliotti is a comic book artist and illustrator. In addition to *Teen Titans Go!*, he has also worked on *He-Man and the Masters of the Universe*, *Sensation Comics Featuring Wonder Woman*, and many other comics.

GLOSSARY

appreciate (uh-PREE-shee-ate)—to value someone or something

cagey (KAY-jee)—cautious or wary

calculate (KAL-kyuh-layt)—to find a solution by using math

commentary (KOM-uhn-ter-ee)—a description of and comments about an event

concentration (kahn-suhn-TRAY-shuhn)—the ability to pay careful attention

deductive (di-DUHK-tiv)—relating to the ability to figure something out based on clues

deliberately (duh-LIB-ur-uht-lee)—on purpose

disqualify (dis-KWAHL-uh-fy)—to prevent someone from taking part in or winning an activity

ignore (ig-NOR)—to take no notice of something

intimidate (in-TIM-uh-date)—to threaten in order to force certain behavior

opposable (uh-POZE-ah-bul)—related to being able to move the thumb toward and touch the other fingers of the same hand

physique (fiz-EEK)—the size and shape of a person's body

pivotal (PIV-uh-tahl)—of great importance to the success of something

ritual (RICH-oo-uhl)—an action performed as part of a social custom

sonic (SON-ik)—having to do with sound waves

species (SPEE-sheez)—a group of animals with similar features

starch (STARCH)—to stiffen clothing with a powder or spray made from starch

tension (TEN-shuhn)—a feeling of worry, nervousness, or suspense

trapeze (tra-PEEZ)—a horizontal bar hanging from two ropes, usually at a circus

unbiased (uhn-BYE-uhst)—not favoring one person or point of view over another

withering (WITH-uhr-ing)—related to a look that is meant to make someone feel embarrassed or foolish

VISUAL QUESTIONS & WRITING PROMPTS

1. How is Raven helping Cyborg in this panel? Where do you think he goes next?

2. A worm's eye perspective shows a scene from the ground up. Why did the illustrator use a worm's eye perspective here? What does it tell you about what lies ahead for Robin?

3. Has Starfire ever played Go Fish before? Explain why you think she has or hasn't based on this panel.

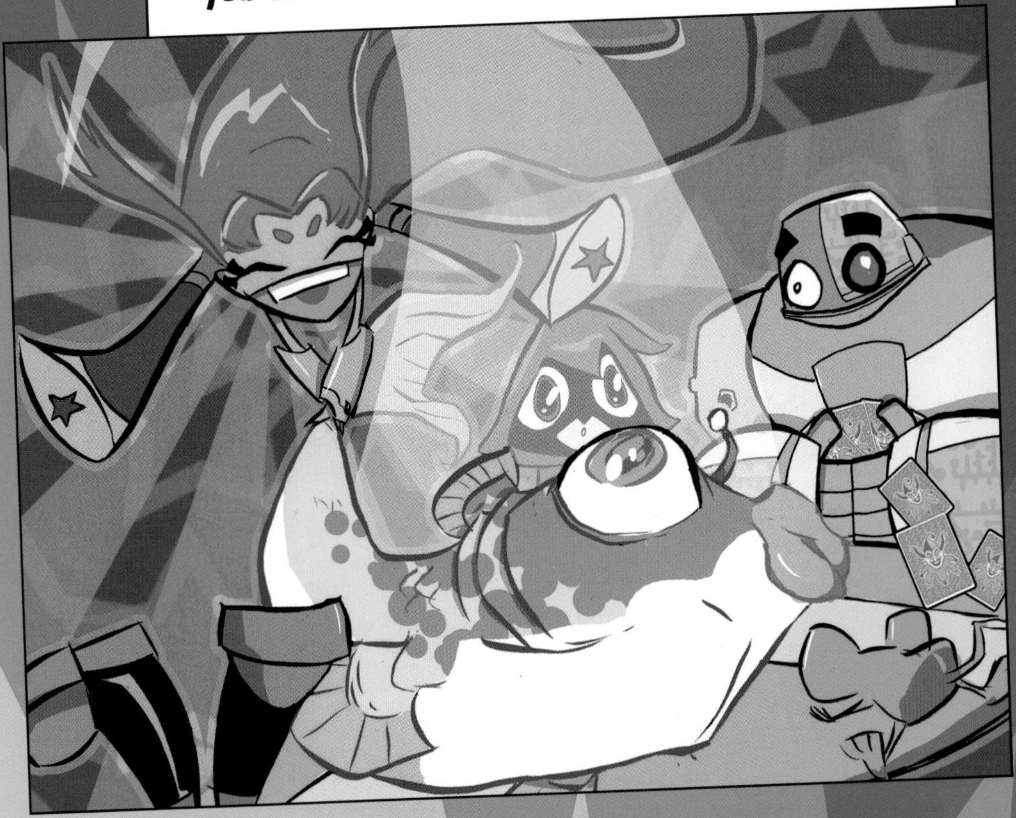

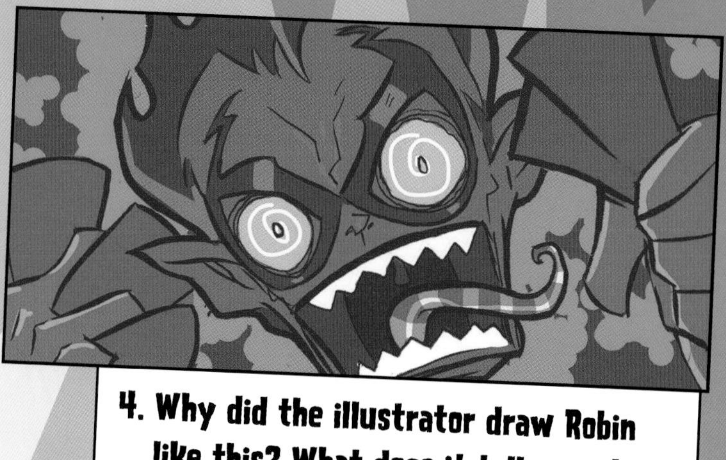

4. Why did the illustrator draw Robin like this? What does it tell you about how the Teen Titan is feeling?

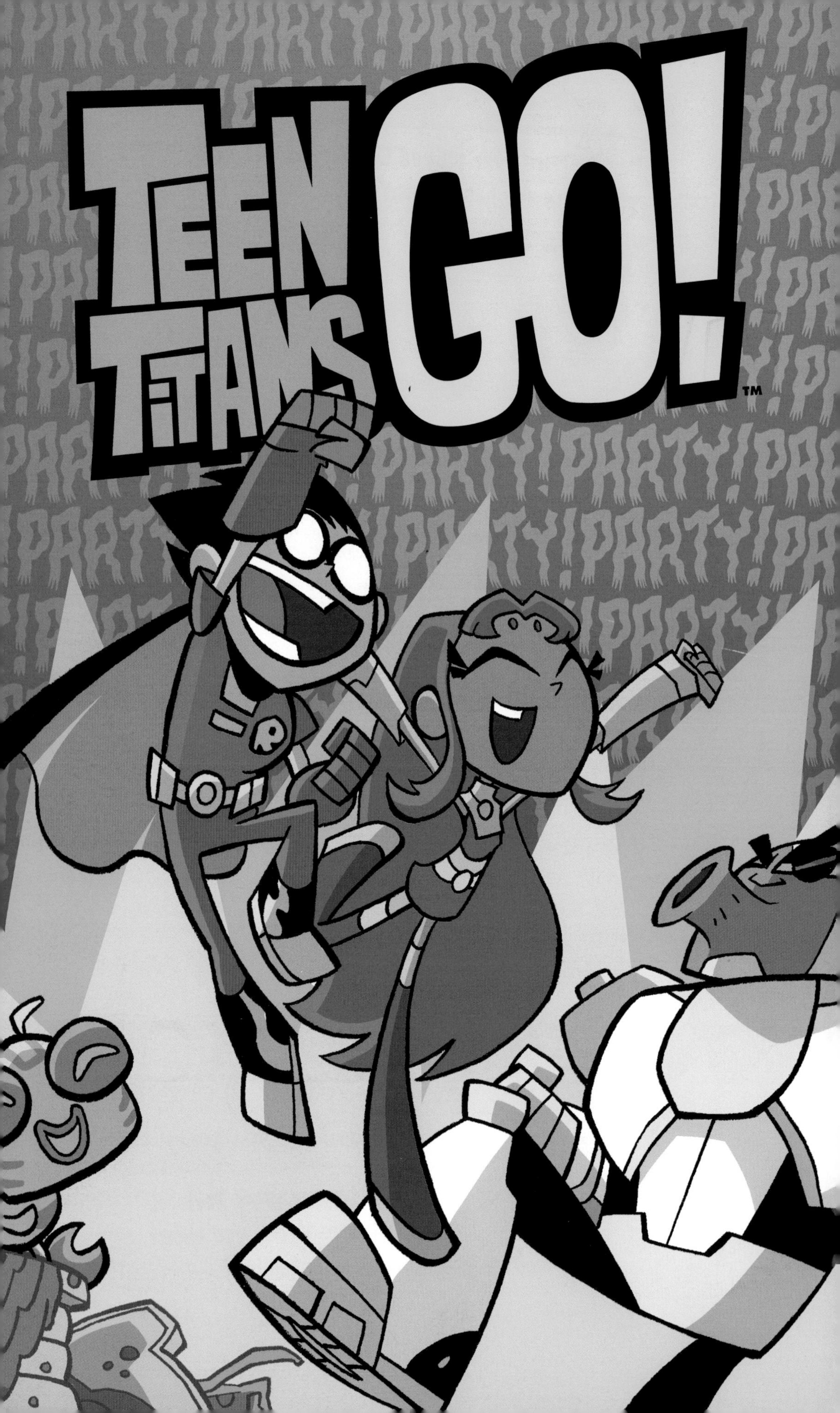
TEEN TITANS GO!™
PARTY! PARTY!

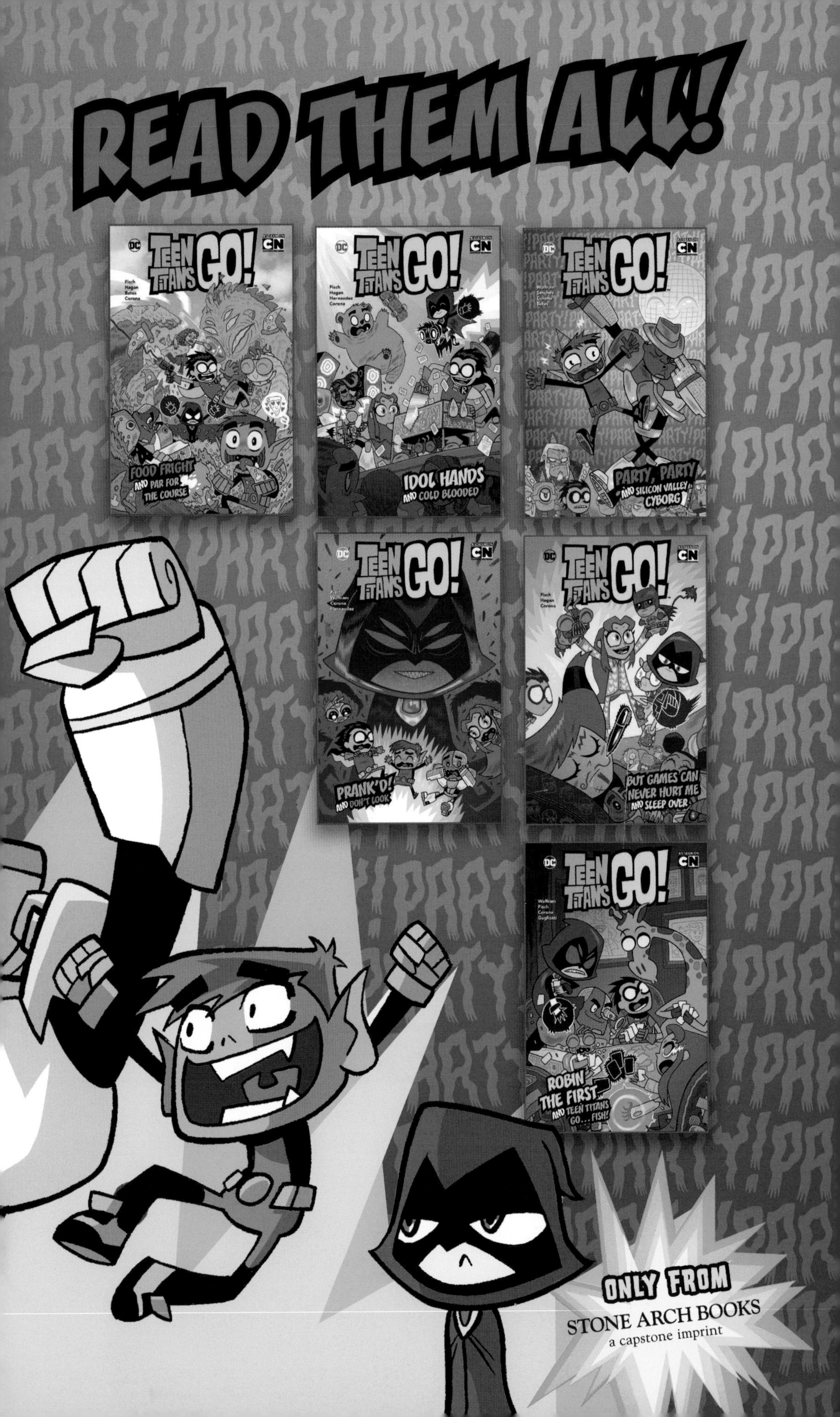
READ THEM ALL!
TEEN TITANS GO!
FOOD FRIGHT AND PAR FOR THE COURSE
IDOL HANDS AND COLD BLOODED
PARTY, PARTY AND SILICON VALLEY CYBORG
PRANK'D! AND DON'T LOOK
BUT GAMES CAN NEVER HURT ME AND SLEEP OVER
ROBIN THE FIRST AND TEEN TITANS GO... FISH!
ONLY FROM
STONE ARCH BOOKS
a capstone imprint

TEEN TITANS GO!™